Clancy
&
Millie
and the
Very
Fine
House

For Amy and Jo and No 11—LG

For Sendo—FB

Little Hare Books
8/21 Mary Street, Surry Hills
NSW 2010 AUSTRALIA

www.littleharebooks.com

Text copyright © Libby Gleeson 2009
Illustrations copyright © Freya Blackwood 2009

First published 2009
Reprinted 2009

National Library of Australia
Cataloguing-in-Publication entry

Gleeson, Libby, 1950-
Clancy and Millie and the very fine house / Libby Gleeson ;
illustrator, Freya Blackwood.
9781921541193
Moving--Household--Juvenile fiction.
Blackwood, Freya.
A823.3

Designed by Vida & Luke Kelly
Produced by Pica Digital, Singapore
Printed by Everbest Printing (Guangzhou) Co. Ltd
Printed in Nansha, Guangdong, China, October 2009

6 5 4 3 2

Clancy
&
Millie
and the
Very
Fine
House

Libby Gleeson
Freya Blackwood

LITTLE 🐇 HARE
www.littleharebooks.com

Clancy has moved from this house

… to this house.

'I love my new home,' says Clancy's mother.
'It's the best house.'

'It's a very fine dwelling,' says Clancy's father.

'It's too big,' whispers Clancy.

Clancy's mother leads him from room to room.

'See this shiny new kitchen,' she says. 'It's much better than the old one.'

Clancy remembers the cubby house under the table.

'And this lovely lounge-room. It's much better than the old one.'

Clancy remembers
the fire in the fireplace.

'And your big comfortable bedroom,' says his mother.
'It's much better than the old one.'

Clancy remembers the skylight
and the moon.

'It's too big,' he says, but she is
already gone.

Clancy goes outside.

He kicks at the sticks and stones
that lie on the path.

He flops down
and watches a fat snail
creep back into its shell.

Then he goes to the boxes.

There are big ones and small ones,
fat ones and thin ones, plain ones and fancy ones.

There is the box from the fridge
and one from the washing machine.

There are boxes that brought
the cushions and the carpets,
the tools and the toys, the bath things
and the books.

Clancy pushes them
and pokes them.

He crawls under
one and sits inside
another.

Then he hears a voice.

'Can I play too?'

A girl climbs over the fence
and lands beside him.

'I'm Millie,' she says. 'What's your name?'

'Clancy.'

They build a tower so tall it topples over

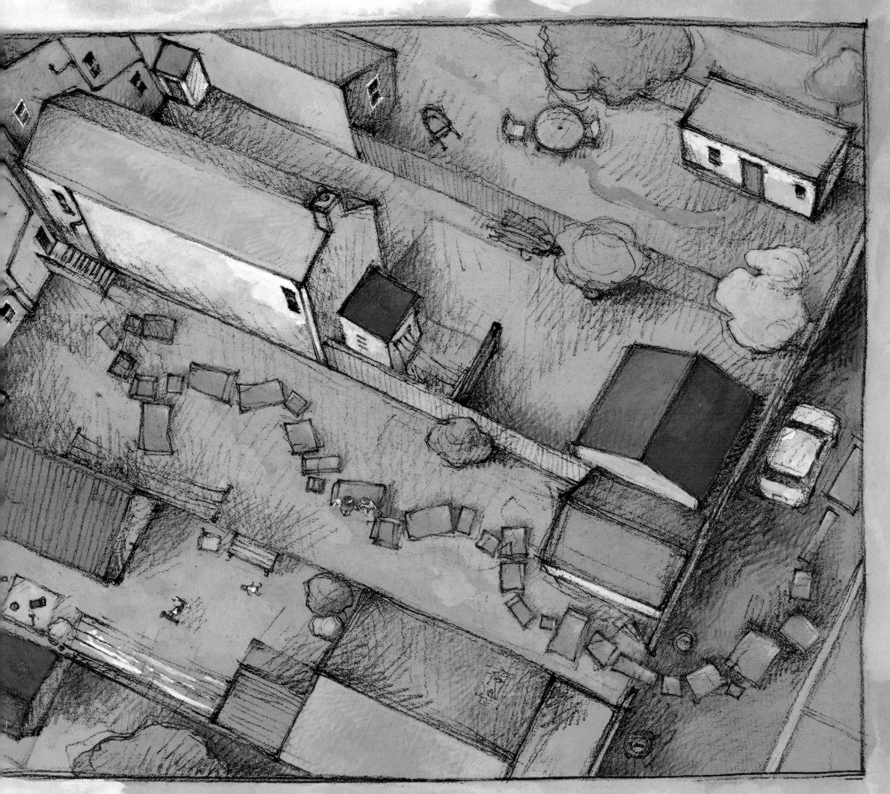

and a train so long it runs out of the yard.

'Now let's build a house,' says Clancy.
'I must be the first little pig
and you must be the big bad wolf
and you're going to huff and puff
and blow my house down.'

And she does.

'Now it's my turn,' says Millie.

'I must be the second little pig
and you must be the big bad wolf
and you're going to huff and puff
and blow my house down.'

And he does.

'Now,' says Clancy, 'I'm the third little pig and this is
my house of bricks and the big bad wolf can't get us.

Not even if it huffs and it puffs till it bursts.'

'It's the best house,' says Millie.

'It's a very fine dwelling,'
says Clancy.